there's a DOLPHIN in the GRAND CANAL!

John Bemelmans Marciano

VIKING

Imagine a city in the middle of the sea. The roads are made of water, and the people use boats the way we use cars. They have water taxis and water buses, boats to deliver the mail and pick up the trash, and boats with sirens for the police and firefighters. But most of all they have gondolas—long, thin boats you will find nowhere else.

The waterways here are called canals. The gondola you see below is riding on the largest of these, which snakes through the city like a backward S. It is called the Grand Canal, and the city you are imagining is Venice.

In a quiet corner of Venice, overlooking a little canal, sits the Caffè Buca. Let's open the door and meet Mamma Buca, Papa Buca, and their son, Luca Buca. Poor kid—look at him, so bored and lonely, stuck in here all summer with his parents. His friends are lucky; they are at the beach or in the mountains or off visiting cousins in other countries.

Every day at two o'clock, the caffè closed for a couple of hours so the family could have a break. Starting at noon, Luca began asking his mother if he could leave early. "Can I please go now?"

"Not until your father says you can."

Finally, at five minutes to one, Papa said, "Okay, Luca, you are free to go out and play."

Luca kissed his mamma good-bye and made for the door. He hoped it was raining out, or at least cloudy, because why should everyone else be having fun when he wasn't having any?

But no, the sky was filled with perfectly hideous sun.

basta, mamma!

Luca started toward the Grand Canal, as he did every
afternoon. Unfortunately, to get there he had to walk through . . .

St. Mark's Square, the most crowded place on earth.

"What are all these people thinking? Coming to Venice from around the world, and for what? To take a ride in a gondola and look at a bunch of stupid old buildings! The last time something exciting happened here was a thousand years ago."

Luca sat on the steps that led down to the water and watched the boats go by.

Just when he couldn't have felt any more sorry for himself, Luca got . . .

SPLASHED in the face by a dolphin!

A dolphin? A dolphin in the Grand Canal? It couldn't be, but there a dolphin was, doing a reverse backflip with a corkscrew finish.

Luca yelled for someone—anyone!—to look, but the tourists were too busy looking at their maps and guidebooks and taking photos of each other.

capperi!

He ran *scusi-scusi-scusi* all the way back home.

Luca burst through the door of the caffè. "Mamma! Papa! There's a dolphin in the Grand Canal! You have to come see! He splashed me right in the face—I think he was trying to play with me!"

Papa cleared his throat and said, "The Grand Canal is full of fish. There are:

MULLET

MACKEREL

SEA BASS

BREAM

ANCHOVY

CUTTLEFISH

EEL

SHRIMP

SOLE

SCORPION FISH

SEA HORSE

THREE KINDS OF CLAM

"But there is not now and there has never been a single known species of dolphin!"
Over his father's protests, Luca dragged his parents *scusi-scusi-scusi* through St. Mark's Square right to the spot where he had been splashed, but . . .

there was no dolphin.

They waited five minutes, they waited ten minutes, and then they waited awhile more, but they saw nothing except boats and birds.

"You see, Luca, I was correct," Papa said. "There are absolutely no dolphins in the Grand Canal."

"But I'm telling you, there was a dolphin right here!" Luca said.

"And I'm sure it was a very nice dolphin too, dear," Mamma said.

So guess who showed up after Mamma and Papa turned around and left for the caffè?

"Stop! Look! Come back!" Luca yelled, but his parents were too far away to hear.

"I've been waiting for you forever!" Luca told the dolphin.

Enh-enh-enh! the dolphin laughed.

ASPETTA!

"Don't laugh at me, you big dumb fish," Luca said, shaking a fist at him.

The dolphin (not a fish at all, but a mammal, the same as Luca) shook a flipper back.

"Stop making fun of me!" Luca yelled.

He was so mad that he never saw what's coming on the next page.

Luca leaned too far over the edge, and he slipped

OOPS!

right off the step

but with a flick and

SPLASH!

and into the sea,

a flip,

Luca landed on the dolphin's back, and they took off . . . ZIP!

Luca held on for dear life, then held his breath, then shouted out with joy, "Go!"

But when they got to the bridge
at Rialto, Luca yelled, "Stop!"

The dolphin didn't, and they sailed right through its arches.

With a soft whoosh,
they flew into this
woman's laundry.

SAN MARCO ‹‹

PER RIALTO ››

"What is everyone making such a fuss about?"
Mamma asked.

"Oh you know these tourists," Papa said.
"There's probably a flock of pigeons taking off or some such nonsense."

Even the dolphin was surprised when he made it
up *up* over the Bridge of Sighs . . .

but not half as much as these folks on the other side.

Luca's parents were almost back to the caffè.

"I tell you," Papa said, "that boy daydreams too much. Dolphins! In the Grand Canal! What will it be next? Camels on the Rialto Bridge?"

"Maybe Luca *did* see a dolphin," Mamma said. "You never know."

"Yes I do," Papa sniffed.

Luca?

"That's

a   very   nice   dolphin   you   have,   dear!"

❧ GLOSSARY ❧

ITALIAN

andiamo [on-DYAH-moh]: let's go

aspetta [as-PET-tuh]: wait

basta [BAH-stah]: enough; stop

bravo [BRAH-vo]: hooray, good

capperi [KAP-peh-ree]: wow (literally means "capers")

caspita [KAS-pee-tuh]: gosh

che bella [kay BEL-luh]: how beautiful

ciao [CHOW]: hi

dove sono? [DOH-vay SO-no]: where are they?

eccoli [ECK-koh-lee]: there they are

guarda [GWAR-duh]: look

mamma mia [MAM-muh MEE-uh]: my goodness

o sole mio [oh SO-leh MEE-oh]: oh my sun . . .

    (lyrics from a love song)

polizia [po-lee-TZEE-a]: police

sospiro [sohs-PEER-oh]: sigh

scusi [SKOO-zee]: excuse me

OTHER LANGUAGES

há um golfinho [HA oom gol-FEEN-yo]: it's a dolphin
    (Portuguese)

hoi [HOY]: hi (Dutch)

kimchi [kim-CHEE]: said when a photo is taken (Korean)

mira [ME-rah]: look (Spanish)

ooh la la [ooh-la-LA]: wow (French)

wunderbar [VOON-der-bahr]: amazing (German)

zdorovo [ZDO-ro-vo]: cool (Russian)

❧ AUTHOR'S NOTE ❧

How exactly do you walk around Venice? The question really concerned me. I hoped the canals at least had sidewalks—I didn't want to have to take a boat everywhere.

On arrival, I was relieved to find that Venice does indeed have streets for walking. There are bridges, over five hundred of them, for where the streets cross canals (and lots of watery dead ends for where they don't).

The water, the gondolas, the boats—it was all overwhelming, but expected. What surprised me were the buildings. They were out of fairy tales, from the great castles of the Grand Canal to the small houses on out-of-the way squares. If they paved over every canal, Venice would still be the most beautiful city on earth.

I loved the place immediately. That first trip I began to write and sketch this story, mostly because I wanted an excuse to come back. Which I did, a lot. No place in the city drew me back to it so much as Campo Santa Maria Nova, the little square that sits behind the Chiesa dei Miracoli (the Church of the Miracles, which Mamma and Papa walk around at the end of the book). It attracted me not because it was extraordinary, but for the opposite reason—the square seemed like a place that just happened to be in Venice. It was the perfect spot for the Caffè Buca.

The Caffè Buca does not exist, but it is a mix of places. During my research, I stopped in a lot of caffès and had a lot of espresso. I drank one cup standing in water up to my knee, a perfectly normal thing to do during the *acqua alta*, when Venice floods.

I was very pleased to learn that the great iron fin of the gondola is called a *dolfin* (Venetian dialect for dolphin, which is *delfino* in Italian). Sadly, the dolfins on the gondolas were the only dolphins I ever saw in Venice. However, the animals themselves have been known to enter the Venetian lagoon from time to time, so keep an eye out for one if you go.

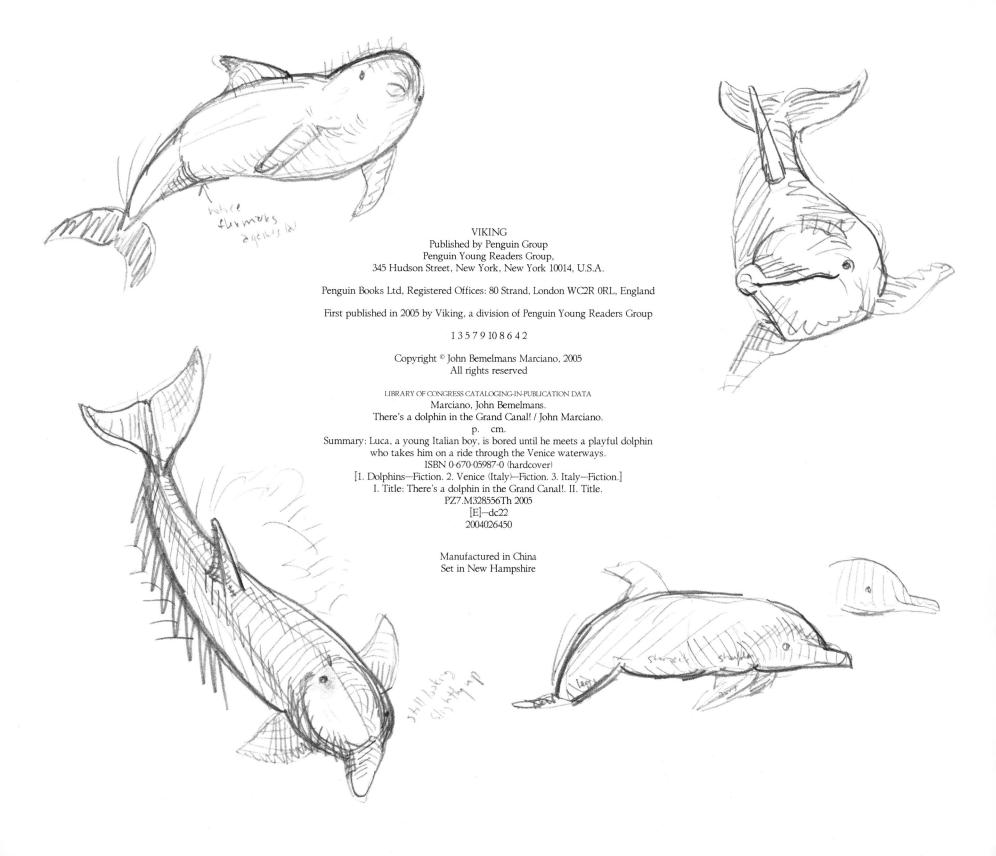

VIKING
Published by Penguin Group
Penguin Young Readers Group,
345 Hudson Street, New York, New York 10014, U.S.A.

Penguin Books Ltd, Registered Offices: 80 Strand, London WC2R 0RL, England

First published in 2005 by Viking, a division of Penguin Young Readers Group

1 3 5 7 9 10 8 6 4 2

Copyright © John Bemelmans Marciano, 2005

LIBRARY OF CONGRESS CATALOGING-IN-PUBLICATION DATA
Marciano, John Bemelmans.
There's a dolphin in the Grand Canal! / John Marciano.
p.   cm.
Summary: Luca, a young Italian boy, is bored until he meets a playful dolphin
who takes him on a ride through the Venice waterways.
ISBN 0-670-05987-0 (hardcover)
[1. Dolphins—Fiction. 2. Venice (Italy)—Fiction. 3. Italy—Fiction.]
I. Title: There's a dolphin in the Grand Canal!. II. Title.
PZ7.M328556Th 2005
[E]—dc22
2004026450

Manufactured in China
Set in New Hampshire